DOWN BRIGHTON.

To Rou

All the best

Olli

You Only Live Nine Times

Other titles by Olli Tooley

In this series

- For Cats' Eyes Only
- Dr Gnaw

  (You don't have to read these first, to enjoy "*You Only Live Nine Times*", but we would like you to buy them anyway)

Time Tunnel Series

- Time Tunnel to Londinium
- Londinium Revisited
- Time Tunnel at the Seaside
- Time Tunnel to West Leighton

Wise Oak Series (Oliver J. Tooley)

- Children of the Wise Oak
- Women of the Wise Oak

  Recommended for older readers, i.e. teenagers and adults.

You Only Live Nine Times

by

Olli Tooley

Illustrated by

Amii James*

With thanks to

David Tubby &

Catherine Newton

*Additional illustrations by Olli Tooley

Edited by Sarah Dawes

Illustrations by Amii James

Printed by Short Run Press

Blue Poppy Publishing

Devon EX34 9HG

info@bluepoppypublishing.co.uk

ISBN-13 978-1-911438-56-4

I would like to thank Year 6 at
Langley Park Primary School, Durham,
for being Beta Readers with Cattitude!

And especially their teacher Lindsay Burnip

Teachers rock!

Chapter 1

Beep ... beep ... beep ... Felix hated hospitals. He hated the smell of bleach and sickness, the oppressive heat, the constant activity going on around him that was not centred on him. Today, at least, that last wasn't a problem, because for once all the activity *was* centred on him. He was lying in bed covered in bandages, with various tubes leading to bags of mysterious-looking fluids.

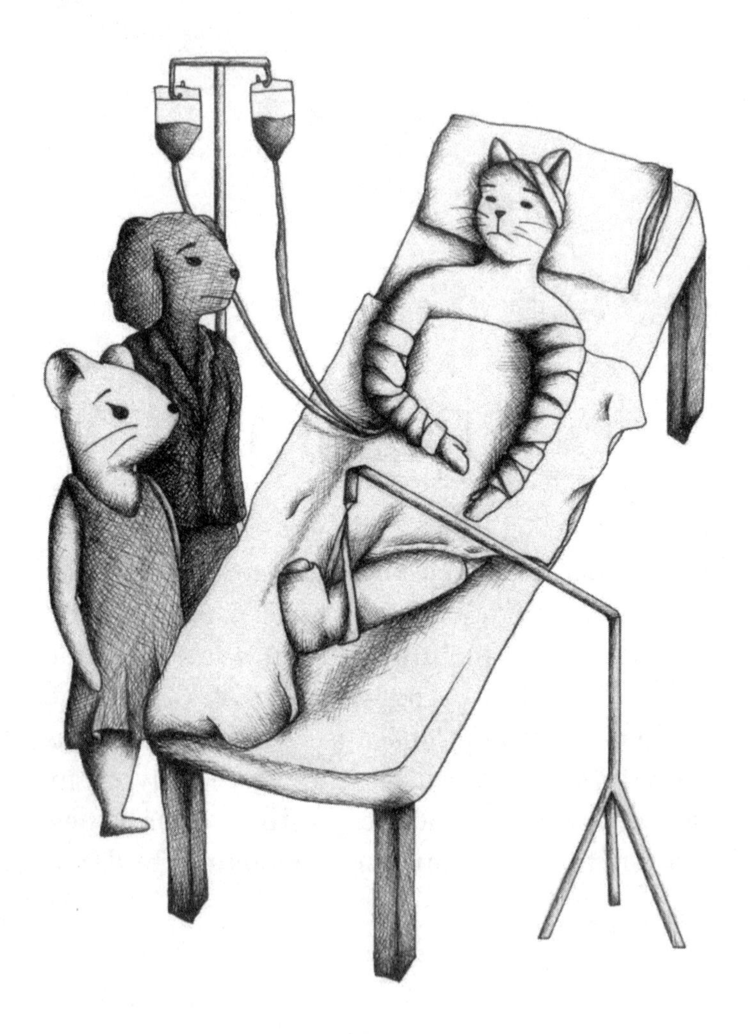

Around the bed stood the important people in his life. His partner, Holly, a keen young spaniel who had achieved the highest pass marks from police school, looked calm but concerned. His boss, M, the stern but efficient mouse who was head of Animal Intelligence Services (AIS for short), looked serious and pensive. Next to her was Felix's mother, the former head of AIS, looking resigned and anxious. Last but not... erm... well anyway, last was Ollie, the dim-witted but lovable owl who was in charge of... well... anything that needed doing at AIS, but which did not require any real intelligence.

"Well, the surgery went well, we've fixed all the broken bones, given him a blood transfusion, and antibiotics for the infection. He's stable now and he should be ready to leave in a week," the doctor explained.

Everyone looked relieved, but then he looked serious for a moment and added, "There's nothing we can do about the paper cut though."

Mrs Whiter sobbed briefly but then pulled herself together. Felix knew the risks when he entered the service and if he had to live with the scars of a paper cut for the rest of his life then she wasn't going to be the one to break down over it.

Felix's eyes flickered open and he took in the four faces gazing down on him. He grinned at them and asked, "Well? Did we catch him?"

"Who?" they all chorused.

"Swifty of course!"

Swifty was a tortoise who, unlike the stereotypical tortoise, was quick and agile and had a knack for escaping capture. He had been running and leaping across buildings attempting to escape from Felix and the AIS team, who were in hot pursuit. Just as Felix was about to catch him, the tortoise pulled a strange-looking mushroom from his pocket. As he ate the mushroom, he got a burst of energy, allowing him to escape. Felix leapt at the empty space where Swifty had been and plummeted from the top of the building. That was the last thing Felix knew about until he had woken up just now in hospital.

"We got him," said Holly. "After he ate that *pawaapu*[1] mushroom he went so fast he ran straight into a brick wall."

---

[1] Publisher's note: This is a fictional mushroom. Some mushrooms are poisonous, and you should not eat them unless they came from a shop or something.

Chapter 2

A week later Felix, with Holly pushing him in a wheelchair, entered Beech House. Holly seemed excited, as though she were bursting to tell Felix something but wasn't allowed to. They went up to the seventh floor and entered M's office. M was paying attention to a small hand-held computer.

"One moment," she said. Then she tapped the screen a couple of times and closed it, looking satisfied with herself.

"Playing Sweetie-Squash?" Felix inquired, with a grin. Sweetie-Squash was an addictive computer game that Sydnee Spider, the IT expert, had got hooked on playing recently.

“Absolutely not,” M responded. “It’s a mental agility testing application actually. Apparently, my IQ is in the top ten percent. But we’re not here to talk about computer games anyway; I want to discuss what we’re going to do about you.”

"I'm gung-ho to get stuck back into some case work. I won't be in this old crusty-wagon for long you know. I can already walk a few steps. Just need to get back on the treadmill, ear to the ground, nose to the grindstone, just like before."

"Yes, well that's all well and good Felix, but the whole department are worried about you. You nearly died in that last incident chasing Swifty."

"But I didn't though, did I? Unless I'm a ghost or something? I'm standing... well, I'm SITTING, right here, living and breathing. Nine lives, remember? Count 'em: NINE."

"Yes, Felix; nine lives indeed. We had Sydnee run some numbers and it looks very much as though you might have used most of them up."

"Nonsense! Can't be," Felix blustered without really having the slightest idea how many near-death experiences he had been through.

"Well," Holly interrupted, "just since I've known you, there's been this recent incident falling off the building, and last year you got knocked down by Swifty on a rocket powered hoverboard and I had to give you CPR."

Felix noticed that Holly looked just a bit too cheerful and he hoped it was for some other reason.

M went on, “Also last year, you were thrown into a shark tank, and beaten up by villains. We’re not sure if that counts as one or two.”

“One! Definitely just one,” Felix insisted. “That shark was never any real threat,” he added, for clarification.

Holly said, “Remember you told me about that long hot summer; you were in a tree, spying on Swifty, but the branch snapped and you fell out of the tree, and hit a beehive on the way down, and it was only because you and the beehive rolled down the hill and off the cliff into the sea that you weren't stung to death; only then you had to escape from a swarm of jellyfish and you had to hold your breath and swim under them and you thought your lungs were going to burst until you managed to get clear?" Holly was laughing as she recounted the story, although she stopped and looked guilty, adding, "I don't suppose it was very funny at the time."

M continued to drive the point home. "There have been a string of other times when, in the line of duty, you came close to death, and your mother tells me that when you were a boy you used to play on the old wasteland near your house and you and a group of your friends were trying to see how many of you could all ride on one bicycle."

Felix pulled a face that was part horror, part pride. Pride, because they had somehow managed to get him and six of his friends all riding on his bike. He had been in the saddle, pedalling, with one friend on the handlebars, one hanging on the back, and two on each side keeping it all in balance. He had managed to ride the bike like this without falling over for quite some distance. The horror was because the story ended with him riding the bike - and all his friends - straight into the canal because he couldn't see where he was going.

(Author's note: Do NOT try this at home.
It is FAR safer trying it outside,
where there is plenty of space.)

(Publisher's note: Ignore the author's note.
- he's an idiot -
Please, do not try this ANYWHERE.)

Felix attempted to argue, "Look, I'm sure I didn't use up my lives on some of those. Sure, I was lucky the last couple of times, but back then when the bike went in the canal we all just got wet and a bit shaken up. Nobody was anywhere close to being killed."

"It's no use Felix, we're taking you off active service until we can be sure."

Felix tried to protest again, "But… What about Holly? She doesn't want to keep switching partners all the time, and she won't want to do some boring desk job."

"Don't worry about me Felix," Holly said, grinning, and almost bursting with excitement.

M smiled. "It's admirable, Felix, that you're more concerned for your partner than for yourself. You seem to have matured a great deal in the last year. You're the ideal person for this job, and Holly will be going with you."

"Going? Going where? Will somebody tell me what's going on? Holly, you look like you're bursting to tell me something."

"I've been told not to say anything until you're told officially, but yes. It's so exciting."

"We're sending you to Japan on a cultural exchange visit. Word has got around about your work at the Akita-Shibu Plaza last year."

M was talking about how Felix had foiled a dastardly plot to hold everyone hostage at a Japanese bank; he and Holly had saved the day.

"We've arranged for you to train at Emoji Castle, with the finest Ninja masters in the world. You will learn the art of self-defence, and if you pass their tests, you will be able to come back and continue in the field. If not, then it's a desk job for you, or early retirement; your choice."

Holly finally released the excitement she had been bottling up and jumped up and down, chanting, "*Watashi wa Nihon ni iku*," over and over again.

Chapter 3

Felix realised he didn't know very much about Japan, so he did what he always did when he needed answers. He headed straight for the library. He only had a day before they were leaving, but he was a quick learner. Cathy, the librarian, was at the desk doing something librarian-y.

"Hello Cathy, can you give me a book on Japan, please? I need to learn everything there is to know about the country in a day."

Cathy burst out laughing, managed to stop just long enough to squeal, "In a day?" and then carried on, doubled up with laughter, "Japan? Everything?" Tears were streaming down her face, and other library users were looking over to see who was making so much noise. Still laughing uproariously, Cathy managed to pull a book called '*An Idiot's Guide to Japan*' from a shelf and hand it to Felix who left with the sound of Cathy's continued laughter echoing after him.

A day or two after Felix and Holly had left for Japan, Ollie was, as usual, having problems with communications.

"Hello? No, the line isn't very good is it? Let's start again; where are you calling from?"

"It's 'Pete's Cakes', the bakers."

"For Pete's sake yourself! Why are you calling from Jamaica?"

"What? It's Pete's Cakes here. A gang of thieves have come in and stolen all the pies."

"A fan of sleeves has come and given you some flies? That doesn't make sense."

"Not flies, PIES - they escaped out the back."

"Flies had a cape on their back? What is this, some sort of superhero insect?"

"They jumped right over a wall; it was six feet!"

"Well, flies are insects, so they would have six feet, but why are you calling AIS?"

"Oh, can't you put me on to someone else please? Someone who isn't a complete and utter..."

The line went dead.

"Well, that's odd," Ollie mused as he put the phone down.

"Anything wrong, Ollie?" It was Jonathan Hart, the white stag who was as efficient as Ollie was incompetent.

"The line just went dead, but it was just some crazy person from Jamaica talking about fans of sleeves taking all the flies. He kept saying 'for Pete's sake' as well."

Jonathan thought hard for a while, then asked, "Pete's sake, Jamaica?"

"Exactly," confirmed Ollie.

Jonathan leaned over the wi-fu [1] communications desk and pressed a button. "HQ to Zulu four-four."

"Zulu four-four responding. Go ahead control."

"It's Jonathan here. Swing by Pete's Cakes, the bakers on Hedge Row, for me please."

---

[1] Wireless Fungal Network. Anyone with a wi-fu device can talk to anyone else, as long as they are close enough to a mushroom. Don't pick or eat mushrooms in the wild. Some of them are poisonous.

"What's the matter, you run out of doughnuts at HQ?"

"Very amusing four-four," Jonathan replied mirthlessly, "It's just a hunch; humour me. Pop in and make sure everything is alright there will you, please?"

"Roger tha…"

But the rest of the sentence was cut off. Jonathan looked at the wi-fu control board with a puzzled expression. He tried another channel, but it soon became obvious that the whole system was dead.

Internal communications were still working so Jonathan contacted Sydnee in the IT department and asked him to find out what was wrong.

Chapter 4

The plane touched down at Neko Toshi airport. Felix had managed to pack everything in his hand luggage, but Holly had a suitcase and also a large trunk. The trunk had caused some annoyance to Felix.

"You can't possibly need that many clothes," he had complained.

Holly was angry, "What makes you think it's all clothes?"

"Well, shoes then."

It was the closest they had come to a serious argument since the first days of their partnership. Eventually, Holly got her way. There were no problems with the excess weight since their luggage went as diplomatic bags anyway.

"I don't think this training will be too hard," Felix boasted, "I already made red belt at the academy, and I think we both know I've had plenty of training at the school of hard knocks. I just hope it doesn't come as too much of a shock to you," he added.

"I think I'll manage," Holly replied.

Holly and Felix emerged from the plane into a field which didn't look so very different from home. Waiting for them was Aki. She was short, very fluffy, a little like a rabbit, but with short rounded ears, and was obviously suffering from a very bad cold.

"Welcome to Japa-*aatchoo!*" she pulled out a red silk handkerchief and blew her nose hard. "My name is Aki ..." she paused to stifle another huge sneeze. Holly was trying to pay close attention to Aki, while simultaneously looking around at all the sights and sounds.

Aki went on, "You must be Herikasu-san and Hori-san... *Aatchoo!*"

Felix looked puzzled, but Holly spoke first, "*Konichiwa,* Aki-san."

"*Ā, anata wa nihongo o hanasu,* Hori-san?"

"Umm... err..." Holly looked panicked.

"You speak Japanese?" Aki translated.

"Oh... umm... not yet. I'd like to learn though," Holly confessed.

"I am to take you to Emoji... *atchoo!* ... Castle."

Aki led the way towards a car which was apparently parked some distance away. Felix was therefore rather surprised when they reached it sooner than he expected; the car wasn't in the distance, just very, very small. Aki opened the door of the tiny little car and slid into the cramped driving seat. Felix called shotgun and folded himself into the front passenger seat. The chair would not go back and his knees were practically on his chin. Although the back seat was also miniscule, Holly was at least able to stretch out sideways across it. Her large trunk had to be strapped on the roof.

Felix tried to make small talk. "So, if you don't mind me asking, Aki, what kind of animal are you? Only, you look a bit like a rabbit, but with shorter ears."

"Yes, I am related to rabbits, but I am a Japanese Pika-aatchoo!"

"A Pikachu?"

"No, not Pikachu, just Pika. I sneezed."

"Oh, yes, of course."

She muttered under her breath, "There's no such animal as a Pikachu anyway."

Chapter 5

Emoji Castle was an amazing place. Felix had imagined a giant old oak on a hilltop overlooking the countryside. Instead, it was a vast network of huge cherry trees, in full blossom, surrounding taller maples, with curved sloping branches. It was a complex of barracks, training grounds, dining rooms, workshops, offices and more. At the centre was a lake filled with ornamental fish, where Aki left them and told them to wait. Felix couldn't help but be impressed. Holly was almost beside herself with excitement. She had been fascinated with Japanese culture and in particular the martial arts. Wanting to share her knowledge, she began to talk about the Shinobi masters who would be training them.

"The Shinobi are amazing!" she gushed.

"Shinobi?" Felix repeated, gazing at the fish swimming around.

"Yes, they are masters of disguise and they can disappear completely into the background."

Felix looked at the nearest fish, which was marked out in iridescent blotches in shades of orange and wondered what sort of background would help it to disappear, or whether it could change colour like a squid.

"Really?" he wondered aloud.

"Yes," Holly continued, unaware that Felix thought she was talking about fish, "they've been around for hundreds of years."

While Felix mused that fish had more probably been around for millions of years, he didn't interrupt.

"In earlier times, they were considered inferior to the Samurai, who looked down on them," said Holly.

Felix scanned the water, trying to spot which fish might be the Samurai, and decided it was probably the deep red one with the long flowing fins that looked like a scarlet wedding dress. Yes, a fish like that would certainly think itself better than all the rest.

"They often used poison, or would fire darts at an enemy."

Felix looked at the fish with renewed respect. They could afford to have bright colours if they were poisonous, he thought.

“These days though, the Shinobi have an almost mythical reputation for martial arts skills, including unarmed combat, sticks or staves, swords, throwing weapons and explosives.”

As Felix listened, he found it hard to marry up the words with the brightly coloured but otherwise completely ordinary fish. Finally, he spoke up, “Wait a minute? How can a fish use a sword?”

Now it was Holly’s turn to be confused.

“What? Who said anything about fish? I was talking about the Shinobi; the Ninja sensei who will be teaching us.”

Felix thought quickly and blustered, “Sorry, I misheard you; I thought you said Schilbe.” [1] He hoped Holly didn’t know anything about fish. Luckily she didn’t, so she continued, “Oh, by the way, there’s something you need to know about. It’s important. The Ninja have one weakness. They are governed by the law of ‘conservation of ninjutsu’.”

“Conversation of what?”

---

[1] Schilbe is a group of fishes similar to catfish.

"Not conversation, con-ser-vation. It means maintaining something."

"I know what conservation is. It's not using plastic straws and stuff; what's the other bit?"

"Ninjutsu is the amount of skill in fighting that is available to go around in any given situation. Nobody has ever explained why, but there is only so much of it, and it is always spread out evenly between two opposing forces."

"So, you're saying if it's a straight fight between a whole pack of vicious dogs in a rough bar, against one cool cat, then the cool cat will always win?"

"Well, not always, but if the cat is trained then he has as good a chance as the dogs, even though it looks like he should lose."

Felix thought about this for a moment then said, "Yep, that makes perfect sense to me."

Chapter 6

Meanwhile, back at AIS they had two major problems.

One was to do with communications. The wi-fu network was still down and nobody could trace the fault. It wasn't just in Wilder Wood but had affected countries around the world. All over Europe, Russia, America and beyond, the type of mushroom which carried the wi-fu signals had been all but wiped out by a mystery virus.

The other problem had been building over some time and also involved a mushroom, but this one was different. Gabby had identified it as a *pawaapu* a rare species known only in Japan.

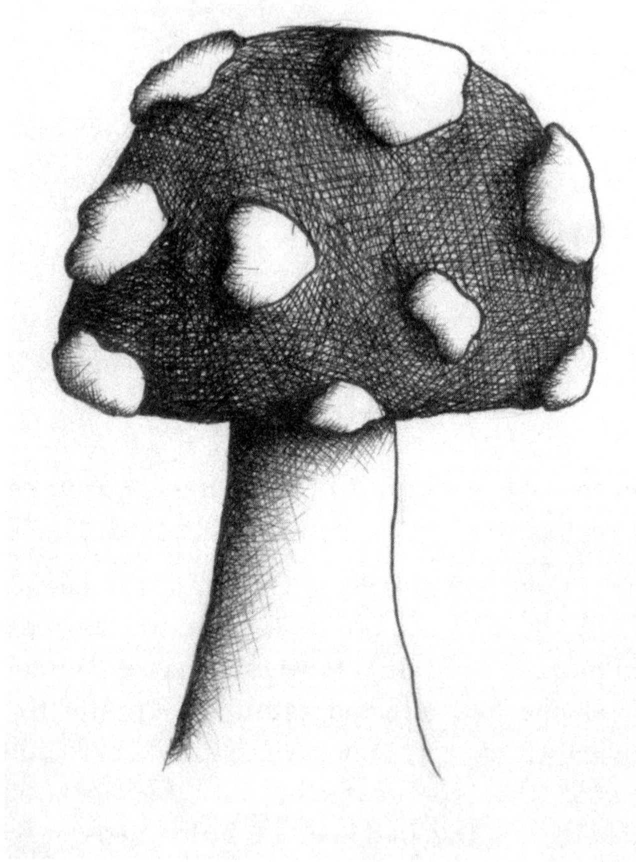

When eaten, it would give a sudden boost of energy for a very short time. [1] Somehow, criminals had got hold of large

[1] Publisher's note: There is no mushroom, in real life, that will give you super powers. There are many which will make you very sick, and some which will kill you.

supplies of this and were using its power-up to help them evade capture. Swifty had used one, causing Felix to fall and hurt himself, and the gang who stole all the pies from Pete's Cakes had used them to jump over a six-foot-high wall. Later, they ate all the pies and were caught while sleeping it off.

AIS were run ragged, chasing after speedy villains and having to use pigeons to carry messages. It was especially difficult without their top agents Felix and Holly.

The wi-fu virus caused a lot of international tension, with America and Russia blaming each other and everyone else taking sides as usual. But Sydnee and Gabby worked together on isolating the virus and eventually concluded that only the Japanese, who had invented the wi-fu system in the first place, could have developed the virus. Gradually, as Russia and America stood down their rows of catapults designed to fire off thousands of exploding coconuts, all the eyes of the world began to focus on Japan.

Emperor Tanaka, a wise and intelligent tiger, denied all knowledge of the virus. He assured the rest of the world that he wanted to know who had done this, just as much as anybody else.

Nobody was really convinced but everyone decided they needed to investigate further.

Chapter 7

As Holly and Felix waited by the lake, a very elderly-looking toad emerged from a grand entrance. He walked slowly, leaning hard on a gnarled wooden cane. As he drew near, Felix could see his robe was very rough plain brown material with no decoration. He looked like the lowliest of servants. The old toad stopped and wheezed a bit before speaking, "*Konichiwa* Herikasu-san and Hori-san." He bowed stiffly and rose again with difficulty.

Felix again wondered who 'Herikasu-san' was but couldn't find a way to ask without being rude. Holly seemed unfazed.

“*Konichiwa*,” Holly said, also bowing, and nudging Felix, who nodded his head and mumbled,

“*Konichiwa*.”

“I have been told to bring you in to the waiting area before you meet your sensei.”

The toad turned and tottered slowly back towards the entrance. Felix and Holly followed, struggling to walk slowly enough not to overtake him.

Inside, there was a long low bench of polished wood. It didn’t look very comfortable but as it seemed they would have to wait for a while, Felix sat down. Both Holly and the toad looked shocked, and Holly gestured urgently to him. As he appeared not to notice, she hissed through clenched teeth, “Get up, you’re sitting on the table!”

Felix leapt to his feet as only a cat can.

“It’s a bit low down for a table isn’t it?” he muttered.

“They sit on the floor,” Holly explained.

The toad interrupted their whispered conversation, “Would you like to take tea?”

Felix was about to say no, but Holly got in first, "That would be most welcome, thank you. I've never seen the tea ceremony."

As their host left, Holly tried to explain a few more things about Japan. Felix was going to need to learn fast if he was not to make any more embarrassing mistakes.

"The Japanese people have a lot of very ancient customs that are different from ours. They don't sit on chairs for meals, but on cushions on the floor, and the tea ceremony is legendary. They have very particular ways of doing everything; it has to be performed in the right order and in the right way, and if you mess it up you have to start again."

"So how do I know what to do? Can I just copy you?" Felix asked.

"No! I've never seen the ceremony myself, I just heard about it. We'll both have to take our cue from him and hope we don't do anything too badly wrong," Holly fretted.

"I don't think it will cause a diplomatic incident if we make fools of ourselves in front of him. He's ancient. I think he must be a servant who just makes the tea and brings guests to see the important people."

"Well, then we get a chance to practice before we meet someone really important, right?" Holly suggested.

"They can't even seem to say my name right," Felix complained.

"That's because there are no sounds like 'Fe-lix' in Japanese," Holly explained.

"And the closest they can manage is Herikasu-san?"

Holly didn't have time to answer before the toad returned and called them through to another room. Here, there was a table beside a charcoal fire, over which was a pot of water, simmering merrily. An ornate polished box stood at one end of the table, there were three tiny cups on delicate saucers - the porcelain so thin you could see daylight through it - and there were cushions on the floor. Their host indicated where Holly and Felix should sit, and then set about preparing the tea. There seemed to be a lot more implements and tools involved, and every movement of their host, as he prepared the drink, was carefully choreographed.

Eventually, he poured out the hot liquid into the eggshell-thin cups. The tea was green, but Felix couldn't easily complain to Holly without being overheard. Both of them watched the old toad carefully for some hint as to what they should do next. He obliged them by now pouring a little of his tea into the saucer and placing the cup next to it.

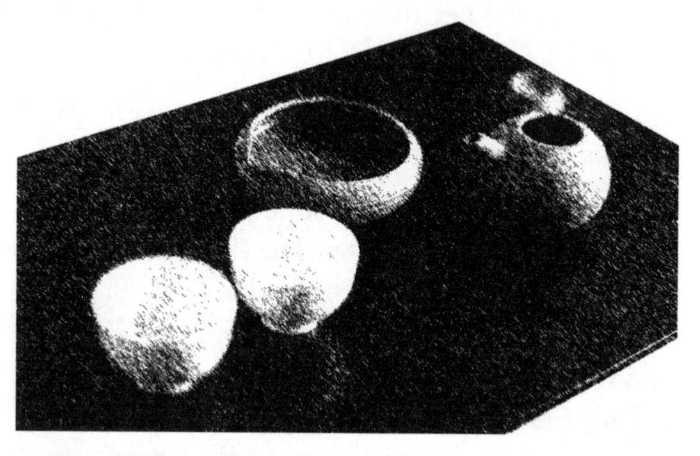

Holly followed his example and poured a little of her tea into her saucer; Felix copied.

Next, the toad took a small jug of creamy milk and poured some of this into his saucer.

Holly and Felix took turns to do the same with their saucers. Neither noticed the toad looking at them with a puzzled expression as they copied his actions.

The toad very carefully picked up the tiny saucer and, hobbling over to the open window, placed it on the ledge. Felix and Holly exchanged confused glances, but they too placed their saucers on the window-ledge alongside the first.

The toad smiled as he said, "It pleases me to see you also care about the small birds. They love to flutter down and drink a little milky tea."

He returned slowly to sit on the floor at the table, while Felix and Holly, feeling a bit silly, did the same. Despite looking a bit odd, the green tea tasted quite good. The old toad cleared away the paraphernalia and showed them to their sleeping quarters. Holly's suitcase and the enormous trunk were already in her room.

Chapter 8

Once left alone, Felix and Holly were able to talk freely again.

"Well, that was embarrassing wasn't it?" Holly said.

"Excruciatingly so," agreed Felix. "So, when do you think our training will begin?" he added.

"I expect someone will take us to our sensei soon. I wonder what he will look like?" Holly wondered.

"Bound to be strong, slim, tall, muscular and wearing an elaborate suit of armour."

"I don't think they wear armour all the time, Felix. Usually, during training, it's just a plain white gi and belt."

"Well yes, but he's going to want to make an impression on us, isn't he? He'll come in wearing his finest armour and weapons, you mark my words."

"Either way, I need to unpack before he gets here."

"Why? Want to impress him with a stunning outfit, do you?"

Holly gave Felix a withering look. "In a way, yes." She opened the trunk and pulled out a thick white canvas gi and a black belt.

"You never said you were a black belt," Felix complained.

"You never asked," she retorted. "Only first dan though," she added.

Felix's eyes widened as she took out a variety of swords, heavy staves, and other exceedingly dangerous-looking items. Last but not least was a complete set of padded body armour including a helmet with a wire face protector.

Felix gasped, "I didn't know you had all that stuff!"

"I haven't really had a chance to use it since the academy. I'm looking forward to taking my training beyond first dan."

Just then, there was a tap on the door and a pangolin entered the room. Tall, muscular, and handsome, he was covered in segmented armour plating which moved perfectly with his body. On his back were a pair of dark sword sheaths and in his hands a number of other lethal-looking weapons. Felix gave Holly a look that said, 'I told you so'. He leapt up and bowed very low before this magnificent warrior.

"*Konichiwa*, sensei. I am Felix, and this is Holly; we are eager to get started with our training."

Holly stood up too and looked at the pangolin, who laughed, "Sensei? Not I Herikasu-san. My name is Tokage and I am not even a senpai, just a humble servant to Senso Dojin, your sensei. I am to take you to him now. Follow me please."

Holly and Felix were astonished; if this heavily armoured pangolin was a mere servant and not even a trainee, then how magnificent would their teacher turn out to be? As they followed along the corridor their hearts quickened with anticipation. Tokage swept the screen door aside and ushered the two agents into a large open room with a circle marked out in rope in the middle. Standing at the centre of the circle was a figure wearing a simple brown robe with a black belt. It took them both a few moments before they realised that this was the ancient old toad.

Chapter 9

It was a few weeks since they had begun their training and it turned out to be quite unlike anything they had imagined. They spent as much time walking among blossom-laden trees as they spent in training, and little of the training involved actual combat situations. Senso Dojin turned out to be deceptively nimble, contrary to his appearance. He could leap higher than either of them, move faster than the eye could follow, and his balance was incredible. But for all his skill, it was his wisdom that was most valued by those around him.

"You have both progressed exceptionally well in only a few weeks. The training you have undergone would have taken most senpai many months. You are almost ready to go out into the field, but first you must know of some of the dangers. Keep away from hornets. They are like wasps but much bigger. Keep well clear of the nests and don't bother them, and you will be fine. There are a few venomous snakes, and the very occasional bear. Apart from them, there is only one serious threat in these parts, and that is the mischievous Tanuki."

"What's a *tanuki*?" Holly asked.

"A *tanuki* is a dog, although it looks a bit like a cross between a badger, a fox and a raccoon, but the mischievous Tanuki, also known as Warui Tanuki, is a trickster and a shapeshifter. He can take on different forms and enjoys nothing more than causing trouble. He heads up a gang called the Organisation of Nefarious Intent, or ONI for short. Up to now they have only been minor trouble to us here, but lately they have begun to create problems worldwide. Word has reached us that a virus has destroyed wi-fu connections in every country, and the source has been traced to Japan."

As they walked through the trees, with blossom swirling down, Felix suddenly noticed a tiger ahead of them. He leapt into a defensive stance, staff at the ready, to defend Holly and Senso Dojin.

Senso Dojin appeared unmoved.

"Holly, may I introduce Ten'nō Dōbutsu? He is our emperor."

He bowed so low that his forehead touched the ground; there was a slight creaking as he stood up straight again. Both Felix and Holly followed suit and bowed as low as they could.

The emperor acknowledged them with a brief nod before saying, "I understand that you are the top agents from AIS, and you have been training here under Senso Dojin."

"Yes, that's right your… emperor-ness?" replied Felix.

The tiger turned to Senso Dojin. "Are they ready to go up against the ONI?"

"They need more time Ten'nō."

"Time is one thing we don't have. The rest of the world think that I authorised the attacks on their wi-fu. Only if we can prove that it was Warui Tanuki, and somehow stop him, can we hope to prove our innocence."

"Then let me send a force in to deal with him."

"*Īe,*[1] I am certain they have infiltrated our organisation. They know all our top agents. I think this is the only way - if Felix and Holly are willing?" The emperor turned to them, eyebrows raised. "There would of course be great rewards for you - and your organisation - should you succeed. However, should you fail..."

Felix knew from experience that the unspoken words here were, 'you face certain death.' This didn't worry him, since he had faced certain death several times before.

"Well, I'm game, but it sounds risky. I can't speak for young Holly here," he said.

"I would be willing to go, but Felix is under strict orders not to go on any active missions until he has passed the utmost test of this dojo," Holly pointed out.

Felix looked at Holly as though she had just stuck a knife in his back.

---

[1] Pronounced *ee-yeh* - Japanese for 'no'.

"Snitch!" he hissed.

Holly ignored him, "He has used up his nine lives. The next time is for real."

"She doesn't know what she's talking about. Sure, I've faced certain death a few times, but not nine. Nothing like nine. Can't be more than six times. Six or seven at most. Definitely not more than eight anyway. What's this final test then?"

"You are not ready," Senso Dojin insisted. He spoke to the emperor, "He still has not even mastered *sen-dachi* or *suro-goku*!"

Felix protested, "That's some sort of trick! You have wires in the ceiling or something."

Holly said nothing, although she herself had recently mastered the art of leaping into the air and freezing for a moment, and of attacking in slow motion, for maximum accuracy and impact.

"He lacks faith, and he gets angry when he does not succeed, Ten'nō. He does not have what it takes."

"Try me!" Felix was angry. He didn't want Holly going off on her own against some unknown and super-powerful foe. She would get all the glory.

Senso Dojin looked angry, as he had never done before. “Fine! Tomorrow at dawn, the outdoor dojo. Go and prepare yourself.” He turned and walked away showing no sign of the stiffness they had seen when they first met him. Emperor Ten'nō watched him leave.

“I’ve never seen him angry before,” he said.

“He’s never met Felix before,” Holly replied, only half joking.

Chapter 10

Felix was angry and, for the first time in his life, a bit frightened. It wasn't fear of death, but of failure, that gripped him. All his life he had been the best. He was top in school, the highest pass mark from the academy, and the top agent at AIS.

Then Holly came along and passed out of the academy with even higher marks than him. She had saved his life on their first case together, and now it turned out she was better at martial arts than he was. M didn't trust him. Senso Dojin said he *wasn't ready*! He'd show them. A badger was snuffling about ahead of Felix as he wandered aimlessly in the woods. He leapt at it.

"Gotcha, Warui Tanuki!"

"*Itai! Sore wa itai yo*!" [1] the terrified badger said.

"Don't pretend you can't speak English, Tanuki."

"Who are you calling Tanuki? I'm a badger, and I speak good English. Better than your Japanese!"

"Don't give me that, Tanuki, I know you're a master of disguise!" Felix began pulling at the badger's face, thinking it was a mask."

"*Itai! Itai*! Stop it *oroka neko*![2] I'm a real badger I tell you!"

Felix began to feel as if he could get nothing right. He apologised and let the unfortunate badger go. Then he took out his frustration on a nearby tree, hitting it until his paws hurt, and then beating it with a cane staff until the staff broke. Feeling a lot better, he

---

[1] I think this means "Ouch! You're hurting me." But Japanese is an unusual language, and it could mean "Ouch! I like that. For the purposes of the story, please assume the first translation. It doesn't matter because Felix can't understand him anyway.

[2] "Oroka neko" = "Stupid cat."

began heading back when another badger appeared. Felix ignored it, but then the badger drew a long sword. Felix leapt into a defensive stance but the badger cut downwards, slicing through a rope, and a spring-loaded net wrapped around Felix, lifting him up into the air where he dangled, trapped, from the high tree branches.

"What? What's going on? Let me down!"

But the badger just laughed as he shape-shifted to reveal that he was really Warui Tanuki, with reddish fur, and a dark facemask.

"Ha, ha, ha! I haven't seen you around before, but you've really gone *up* in the world, whoever you are."

"Warui Tanuki?" Felix said in disbelief.

"Yes, indeed, Neko-tan. Considering you are all tied up at the moment, you seem to like hanging around a lot!"

"You think you're pretty funny! Let me down this instant!"

Warui Tanuki mocked him, "*Nyan, nyan, nyan*! You are in no position to tell me what to do. Tell me who you are, and I will let you down."

"I'm Felix Whiter. Now..."

"Now, Felix Whiter, you should stay there, I think."

"What? But you said..."

"*Sayonara*, Neko-tan," Tanuki chuckled, as he scampered away into the forest.

As annoyed as Felix was, he thought, *'at least HE can say my name properly.'*

Chapter 11

It was late at night when Holly and Aki began to wonder what had happened to Felix. Neither had seen him and they both agreed he should get a good night's sleep before the test at dawn. Eventually, they went in search of him and found him still dangling from the tree in the rope net. When they were able to stop laughing they cut him down and went back to the castle without further incident.

The next day Felix woke before dawn, dressed in full training gear, and collected his practice weapons before heading to the outdoor dojo with Holly and Aki.

As Felix approached the large clearing in the trees he was astonished to find his old enemy, Swifty the tortoise, was there. Was this the test? He had to catch Swifty? Easy. He had done that plenty of times. Catching Swifty was only half the battle; it was the fact he kept escaping that made him so irritating.

As they got closer, Felix saw that Swifty had apparently brought three friends, but then he realised that this wasn't Swifty at all. There were four tortoises waiting at the dojo, all of whom looked like adolescents, not like Swifty who was middle aged. They looked freakish and appeared armed and ready for battle.

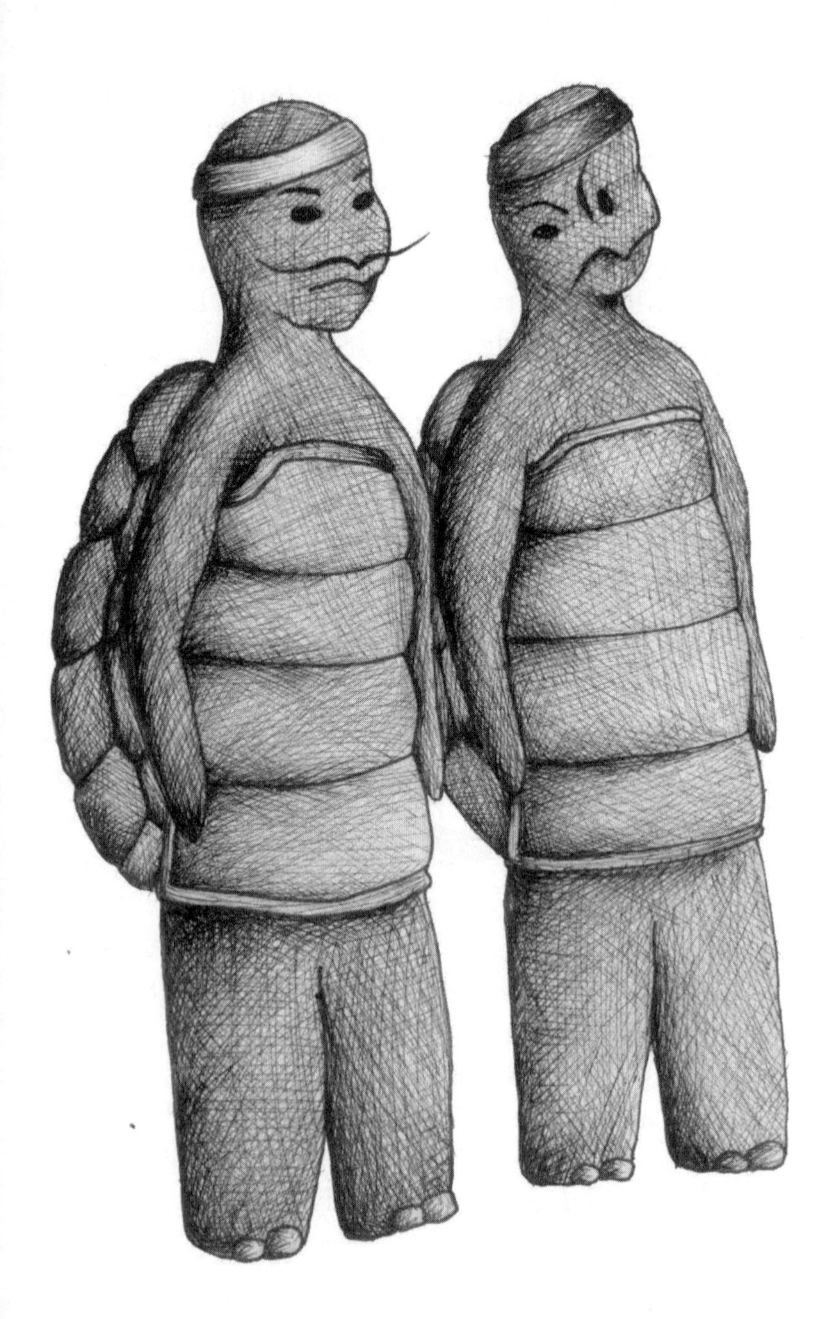

Senso Dojin introduced them one by one.

"Herikasu-san; this is Salvador."

The first tortoise bowed low. He wore a bright yellow headband and had an extraordinary moustache, wider than his face, which ended in two sharp points.

Pablo was introduced next. His headband was blue, and Felix couldn't help noticing that one eye was considerably higher than the other, and that his mouth seemed to be lopsided as well, but he didn't say anything.

The third tortoise was a female named Frida. Her eyebrows were extremely prominent, and they joined in the middle. Her headband was a mass of pink flowers.

Lastly was Vincent, who sported a neat orange beard. He had a matching orange headband which incorporated a large medical pad over one ear.

Senso Dojin explained, "There are three phases to the test. Phase one is that you must fight and defeat these four adolescent freakish Shinobi tortoises."

Felix wasn't entirely paying attention. His mind was occupied with trying to figure out how Senso Dojin had managed to say

‘Salvador’, ‘Pablo’, ‘Frida’, and ‘Vincent’ without apparent difficulty, but still struggled to say ‘Felix’.

The toad continued, “Your task is to remain in the circle, and conscious, until you have defeated all comers. Phase two is a simple test of skill, agility, and quick thinking. *If* you make it to phase three… you face me.”

Felix gulped. He had learned, from his weeks of training, that the ancient toad was anything but old and feeble, as he had seemed on the first day they arrived.

Chapter 12

If he was to remain in the circle, Felix decided the centre was the best place to be. All he had to do was concentrate on each phase as it came. The four adolescent freakish Shinobi tortoises stood around him and each bowed low in turn as Felix turned and bowed to each of them. With the formalities over, he immediately took on a defensive stance, trying to keep an eye on all four attackers at once. They didn't attack immediately, and he swung his cane swords around in a series of sweeping motions, spinning like a top. Each of the four opponents at once performed a spectacular backflip, spinning high above Felix and landing at the edge of the circle. Felix waited to see what their next move would be.

Pablo attacked first, leaping into the air and performing a series of somersaults, firing off several small explosions which Felix avoided easily. He then counterattacked with an impressive backflip of his own, which allowed him to knock Pablo off balance, causing him to land painfully on his back.

Salvador was next. His attack was slower and Felix was quick to counterattack with a swipe of his cane sword, but as he swung, the sword suddenly went limp and flopped down as though it were made of polythene. He whipped out his nunchaku - two heavy wooden sticks attached by a chain - but as he went to attack, the chain suddenly went stiff and he missed the target. Salvador spun round and placed a series of kicks against Felix's chest, but Felix was just able to catch one flying foot and flip his opponent away.

Now Frida began her attack. As she flew through the air Felix dodged nimbly, but then she stopped in mid-air. A perfect *sen-dachi*! Felix tried to see where the wires were that must surely be holding her up, yet here, in the outdoor dojo, there was nothing for wires to attach to. His thoughts were interrupted by Frida crashing down into him, having changed direction in mid-air. The wind was knocked out of him and Frida took advantage to deliver a flurry attack. Drawing on reserves of strength he didn't know he had, Felix deflected a blow and redirected Frida's momentum to throw her over his shoulder. Spinning round, he leapt high in the air but, as he was dropping down to deliver a crushing blow, Frida's belt came undone.

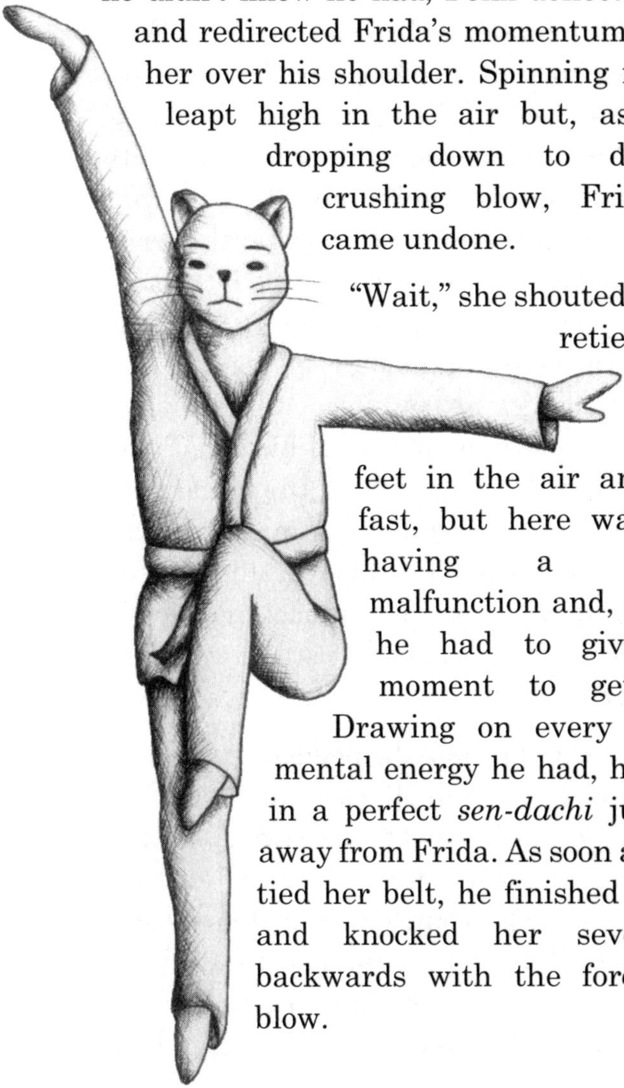

"Wait," she shouted, trying to retie the knot.

Felix was ten feet in the air and falling fast, but here was a lady having a wardrobe malfunction and, somehow, he had to give her a moment to get sorted. Drawing on every ounce of mental energy he had, he stopped in a perfect *sen-dachi* just a foot away from Frida. As soon as she had tied her belt, he finished the move and knocked her several feet backwards with the force of the blow.

'One more,' Felix thought, turning to face the fourth tortoise. Vincent stalked forward slowly, keeping two short staves whirling so fast they became a blur. Felix would have to time his block with incredible speed and accuracy. His attacker drew closer, and Felix chose his moment carefully. With split-second timing, Felix struck and was rewarded with an almighty crack on the wrist from the staff; the second followed through with deadly precision, against Felix's head. He flew backwards and landed on his back. For a few brief moments he could see stars swirling round him and then he shook his head and looked around. He was still in the circle and, unless this was a terrible nightmare, he was still conscious. He leapt to his feet and located Vincent, who was again approaching slowly but surely, the staves still whirling relentlessly.

Felix thought fast: he needed more time. He had managed to pull off a *sen-dachi* against Frida, now he would need to use *suro-goku*, the ability to slow down time to make his attack more accurate. When Vincent was almost close enough to strike, Felix leapt and focused his mind on slowing the whirling sticks, just as Senso Dojin had tried to teach him. Sure enough, for just a brief moment, the blur of motion slowed and Felix could see the sticks clearly. He grabbed both out of the hands of his attacker and landed two feet firmly against the tortoise's shell. As time sped back up, Vincent did a double back somersault landing heavily in the dirt.

Now all four tortoises circled Felix simultaneously. They were going to join forces and attack him at once. Felix looked desperately over at Holly and Aki, who had been willing him on, but he felt that this was surely hopeless. The attack came, and Felix was hit by an almost unbroken series of kicks, hits, and firebombs, bouncing first this way then the other across the circle, landing right on the edge at the feet of Holly. As the four reptiles closed in, he called out, "I can't beat them all at once; they're too strong!"

"Remember conservation of ninjutsu," Holly urged. "Use it to your advantage!"

'Of course,' Felix thought, *'how had I forgotten that?'*

His confidence surged once more and he leapt to his feet. The gang of four were charging him again, even as he stood on the edge of the circle. He waited. They stampeded towards him, but now that there were four of them and only one of him, they were no longer individually as good as they had been when they attacked one by one. Felix waited until he could see the whites of their eyes, then he leapt vertically. Pablo, Salvador, and Vincent all stumbled out of the circle so rapidly that Holly and Aki had to leap to get out of their way too. Frida managed to stop herself but, as Felix dropped back down, he stopped and froze in mid-air at the height of Frida's head. Now he had mastered *sen-dachi* he wanted to show off. With *suro-goki* he spun in slow motion and delivered a blow to Frida that sent her flying over the other three tortoises and he emerged victorious from phase one.

Chapter 13

Felix waited for phase two. Suddenly, from directly above him, a large and odd-shaped green block descended and landed on the ground in the middle of the dojo. Another followed it, this time blue and a different shape. As more blocks dropped they filled up the space in the circle. If this continued, Felix realised, he would be forced out of the circle and it wasn't even a fight. He punched the blocks, but nothing happened. They were stacking up, and there were gaps in between them which meant the space would fill all the more quickly. He started moving the blocks so that they fitted together and filled up the spaces. Suddenly, a line of blocks with no spaces between them disappeared. Felix had a sudden moment of realisation and started to line up the blocks to fill the gaps as they fell. Each time he made a row of four the row disappeared. He kept doing this until there were no more blocks.

'Was that it?' he thought, but then he remembered that now he would face Senso Dojin himself.

The toad stepped into the circle and bowed low before waving his arms around in a series of practiced movements, limbering up. Felix adopted a ready stance and was rewarded by a sudden and furious onslaught of ice balls which buried him in several feet of slush. He swung his staff round, creating a whirlwind which flung the snow and ice around him in all directions, but was then hit by a new attack consisting of fireballs, which Felix dodged by leaping upwards. He held his position in the air as the fire flew beneath him, but the next wave of fireballs was blasted higher, and Felix realised that somehow he must either leap up further, from mid-air, or drop down and hope to avoid being hit. Since he was quite certain the former action was impossible, he dropped, and a fireball spun him violently into a heap on the floor.

He struggled to his feet. Senso Dojin was standing over him. Felix was about to resume the fight when he realised he was outside the circle. He had failed.

Chapter 14

"You fought well, and with honour Felix," Senso Dojin said kindly.

Felix's eyes opened wide. He didn't say anything. He was just astonished that the great master had finally said his name right. He bowed low and managed to whisper the words, "Thank you, Senso Dojin."

Felix spent the next few days continuing his training alongside Holly, and mastering the advanced techniques that would help him pass the test next time. He had moved beyond jealousy of Holly and anger at his own failings. Now he was calm and felt able to relax into the routine. He even spent evenings in the common room with the other trainees and, one night, Frida spotted him.

"Thank you for your honourable conduct during the trial," she said.

"Oh... err... it was nothing," Felix insisted.

Both knew there were no hard feelings over the battle. It would have been dishonourable to have held back in the dojo.

"We're playing *hanafuda*. Do you want to join in?" Frida asked.

"*Hanafuda*?" Felix echoed.

"They're traditional Japanese playing cards," Frida explained.

They dealt Felix in, and he looked with interest at the designs on the cards. On the box were Japanese symbols:

ニャン天堂

"What does the writing say?" Felix asked.

"*Nyan-tien-do*," Salvador responded.

"So, what does that mean?"

"It depends on how you interpret them to some extent," Frida started.

"Let's just say that one translation is 'Cat God Temple'," Pablo interrupted, with a friendly grin.

"I'll take that," Felix laughed.

* * * * *

When they were not training, Holly and Felix went for walks in the forest with Aki the pika.

"You fought incredibly well in the trail, Herikasu-san," Aki said.

Felix thought for some time and then changed the subject.

"Aki, how is it you speak really good English, but you still can't pronounce my name?"

"I don't know."

"Senso Dojin couldn't until after the trial, then suddenly he could."

"I think he always could, but he chose to honour you when you did better than he expected."

Aki looked at Felix to see his reaction, but his answer was cut off as he abruptly disappeared down a hole in the ground. Holly fell in as well, and both agents had completely disappeared. Aki looked down the hole, which had been covered over with sticks and grass, but there was no sign of her friends, just a long tube disappearing into the ground, with the sound of Holly and Felix's yells echoing around and fading to silence.

Aki thought fast. She could either jump down the hole with them or run back for help first. She decided to run back for help, since there would be nobody to help any of them if she wasn't able to.

Chapter 15

Meanwhile, Holly and Felix came to a halt in a confused heap at the bottom of a long chute. They found themselves in a small chamber with a large metal door on one wall, and, very high up on the opposite wall, a barred window. They were in some sort of prison. There was a dim light emanating from the ceiling, a small wooden bench, a bucket, and nothing else. Felix leapt up to the window and clung on to the bars.

"What can you see?" Holly asked.

"Not much. Boots, mostly."

"Boots?"

"Yeah, heavy footwear, reaching above the ankle. Boots."

"I know what boots are! I meant, can you tell anything else from the boots?"

Felix couldn't hold on any longer. He let go of the bars and dropped down. "Take a look yourself," he gasped.

Holly leapt up and scanned the scene.

"Lots of boots. They look like the sort of boots worn by the private army of an evil mastermind," she reported.

"Yes, I thought they looked like some sort of evil minions," agreed Felix.

Holly let go and jumped down. "Definitely got a minion-y look about them," she grumbled.

"Minion-esque," Felix grinned.

"Minion-ish," Holly chuckled.

"Minion-atious!" they both laughed hard, even though there was nothing much to laugh about in their current situation.

Then... "Shh!" they both whispered at once. There were footsteps coming along the corridor outside. They held their breath. The clinking sound of a key, the clunk of a bolt drawing back, the creak of a protesting hinge and two armed guards entered, looking... minion-like.

The guards, both wearing ninja hoods and masks, looked around the cell, which appeared to be empty. As they turned to leave, Holly and Felix dropped from above and knocked them both out.

Chapter 16

It took a few minutes of struggling to pull the red uniforms off the unconscious guards. They looked pretty silly in their long pink underwear.

"Pink?" Felix exclaimed.

"They probably wash everything all together. Red outfits, white underwear. Never a good combination."

They put the red suits on over their own clothes, as they were quite loose. There was a logo on the left chest, a circle with a Japanese character, and the capital letters 'ONI'. The boots were on the large side too, but the important bit was that, with the masks, their faces were covered, so they felt they could pass themselves off without any trouble as long as nobody asked them any tricky questions, such as where the toilets were.

They dragged the guards into a corner of the cell and slipped out, locking the door behind them. In the corridor Felix started sneaking along, until Holly pointed out they would look more suspicious that way.

“I knew that,” Felix said, straightening up and walking boldly towards what looked like a busy area.

All around them there were strange-looking technological devices: flashing lights, buzzing wires, and an installation inside a glass case which appeared to consist of a number of large green rock crystals. Monorails led off in various directions and occasionally an open car slid past carrying red-clad passengers. More Ninja minions passed them, either coming the other way or crossing from side corridors, some disappearing into rooms which contained mysterious experiments glowing in assorted colours. Somehow, they were getting away with it; nobody had spotted them or realised they were intruders. The uniforms were a perfect disguise.

Then it happened. Some sort of alarm began wailing. Felix froze, his heart in his throat, but then relief flooded over him as he noticed that, instead of everyone grabbing hold of Holly and him, the red minions were all hurrying in the same direction. He and Holly both realised they would have to go with the flow or they would stand out like a flea on a bald patch. They joined the general movement towards an unknown destination. As hundreds of red uniforms converged on a wide-open area dominated by a raised stage, Felix recognised Warui Tanuki. When everyone was assembled in the great hall, Warui Tanuki raised his hand, the lights dimmed and a screen flickered into life.

The *tanuki* began explaining his evil plans, illustrated by images shown on the screen. Although he spoke Japanese, it seemed that the minions were of various nationalities, and there were subtitles in several languages. He explained how the wi-fu virus had knocked out communications worldwide, and the sale of *pawaapu* mushrooms[1] to petty criminals had helped finance the final part of his fiendish plan.

---

[1] Publisher's note: I don't know if we've mentioned this, but it's a really bad idea to eat any kind of mushroom unless you are sure that it is safe. Lots of wild mushrooms are poisonous and only an expert can tell which is which. The simplest way to tell is, if it comes from a bag or box in the fridge, it's probably safe (although even then you should make sure they haven't been in there so long they've gone slimy) If you picked it in the woods, then you should probably just chuck it away.... And wash your hands as well!

This plan involved a machine which looked like a very large and highly polished weapon which, when given sufficient power from something called *nise-no-zairyō*[2] (there didn't seem to be a translation) would be capable of destroying entire forests and boiling away oceans. Felix decided that he did not need to see any more before he took action.

With a glance at Holly, he launched himself into a huge somersault over the heads of the red-suits in front of him and onto the stage. He pulled off his mask and shouted, "Not so fast, Warui Tanuki!"

"Felix! So, you escaped from my little trap, did you? Well this time I won't be so merciful. Get him!" he ordered his nearest guards.

Holly sighed and thought, *'a cat never changes its whiskers'*. She then removed her own mask and executed a similar leap, to land with her back to Felix. Together they faced a closing circle of attackers.

---

[2] For your benefit, this roughly translates as 'fake material' and is a joke reference to the TV trope 'Phlebotinum'. None of this has been checked by a Japanese person!

She mouthed to Felix, “Don’t forget conservation of ninjutsu.”

“I haven’t. That’s why I knew I would be alright attacking them all on my own,” he responded. “In fact, by leaping in to help me, you’ve made my job that much harder.”

“Wait, what? That’s not how it works! You can still get hurt when you’re outnumbered.”

“Oh!”

And with that worrying comment, there was no more time for talking as they parried a series of attacks from the red Ninjas. Meanwhile, it looked like Warui Tanuki was getting away, running up a staircase and leaping onto a cart of the monorail. As Felix and Holly fought, however, they noticed a small red minion run after Tanuki and leap across an impossible gap to grab hold of the side of the cart. Between blocking and striking back at their attackers, they saw the red Ninja’s hood and face mask come off, revealing it to be none other than Aki. Neither Holly nor Felix had actually seen the pika fight before but now was not the time to watch, as they were still battling for their lives.

Eventually, they managed to clear the main raised area and had a precious few seconds to get their breath back. However, there was still a sea of minions below them and no way to get out without fighting the whole lot.

"Conservation of ninjutsu or not, we're not going to make it, are we?" Felix asked.

"Probably not," admitted Holly.

"In that case, I'd like to say..."

"Yes?"

Chapter 17

"Hold everything!" An American voice, from among the massed ranks of red, rang out like a bellowing moose in a sea of sheep. A faceless warrior reached up and pulled off his mask.

"I'm Special Agent Tom Katzenburger of the F.B.I. That's the Feline Bureau of Investigations, in case you're wondering, and I'm not gonna stand around and let my British colleagues get their butts whooped by some red menace."

He took up a defensive stance as several of those surrounding him turned their attention to him.

Before the fighting even began in that part of the room, another voice spoke up; this time, it was French.

« Aussi, je suis Agent Spéciale Monsieur Lecoq, Direction Centrale de la Poulet Judiciaire, à votre service ! »[1]

From another point in the room a distinctively British voice piped up.

"What ho, chaps! Vincent Blue[2], Mouse Intelligence Five, and this is Ashleigh Kidderton, we're both up for a good scrap too."

Nearby, another plummy English accent called out, "I say, Vinnie? Ash? I didn't know MI5 were onto this." The new voice introduced himself, "Rudy Leicester, and Katie Lavender! MI6., Got your backs chaps."

"Good to have you on board Katie! Red!"

More agents were now revealing their presence all over the room. The Canine Intelligence Agency (CIA) were there, Israel

---

[1] This is a very clever joke because in France, a mildly rude word for police is poulet which means chicken. In French writing they don't use "..." for speech, but instead they use chevrons. «...» so this is not a mistake.

[2] All the mouse names are a reference to something, but you will just have to work it out for yourself. Or ask at your nearest cheese shop.

had sent Mouse-aid, the Australians were represented by the Defence Intelligence National Government Organisation (DINGO), a squad from the Special Animal Service (SAS) were there along with the *Bundeskatzenrams* from Germany, and a pair of squirrels who declared they were from Italy's *Agenzia Informazioni Scoiattolo Esterna.* Felix noticed Frida, Pablo, Salvador, and Vincent were there as well. Aki had brought reinforcements.

Those minions who had not been knocked out and stuffed into various broom cupboards by the world's secret agents watched in horror as more and more of them removed masks and declared themselves on the side of the good guys. Before any proper fighting could resume, the tables had completely turned, and the good guys massively outnumbered the baddies. Luckily for Felix and his new allies, the conservation of ninjutsu effect was slow to readjust, so they made short work of the resistance and had everybody tied up in double-quick time.

Chapter 18

Everyone was celebrating and congratulating themselves. Felix and Holly were the centre of attention, as agents from every country in the world wanted to shake their hands for being the first to break cover. Gradually, the whole story became clear: every animal agency around the world had managed to infiltrate ONI, but since none of them communicated with each other, not even agencies from the same country, none of them knew that all the others were there too. Hundreds of agents had been going around dressed in the red minion suits, trying to find a suitable way to defeat

Warui Tanuki and foil his plans, but it was only when Felix and Holly had unmasked that the rest of them felt they had no choice but to come to their assistance. While Felix was enjoying all this adulation, there was a nagging worry at the back of his mind. Suddenly he shouted, “Aki!”

“Aki!” Holly echoed.

Everyone else looked confused.

“Our friend Aki, the pika, went after Warui Tanuki on the monorail. We have to help her,” Felix explained.

Everyone leapt back into action, pouring over the monorail and rushing along corridors and up staircases in search of the brave little pika and the evil mastermind. Eventually, they found them and had them surrounded - but there was one problem. Tanuki had shapeshifted into the exact same form as Aki. They were locked in deadly combat, and nobody knew which was the heroine, Aki, and which was the villain, Tanuki. They could not interfere with the fight unless they could be sure.

Felix tried calling Aki’s name, but both turned around very briefly, acknowledging him with a glance, but not taking their eyes off each other as they continued to parry and attack. It was closely matched. Whichever one was Aki, Felix realised she was a superb fighter. He tried a different tack, calling Tanuki's name, but neither responded. Tanuki wasn't going to fall for such a simple trick.

One of the Akis - Felix decided she was Aki A - leapt up and froze in mid-air, then shot down at tremendous speed, while the other Aki - Aki B - dodged with even greater speed, and spun round knocking Aki A sideways and onto her back, winded. It all happened so quickly Felix could scarcely follow it.

Aki A looked across and pleaded, "Help me Felix! Tanuki is too strong!"

As she said this, Aki B leapt again into the air. Summoning up the last of her strength, Aki A rolled out of the way of the attack, gasping for breath. Aki B rolled right to the feet of Felix, who helped her up, and then delivered the knock-out blow to Aki A, who was still on the floor trying to get her breath back.

As soon as Felix has done this, she transformed back into the shape of Tanuki, and everyone cheered. The real Aki gasped.

"How did you know that wasn't me, Herikasu-san?" she protested.

"You just answered your own question, Aki. He said my name properly; you have never been able to," Felix smiled.

And at that everyone cheered.

Chapter 19

Back in Wilder Wood, there was a big celebration at Beech House. Tables were loaded up with food and the fizzy dandelion juice was flowing. Felix was the centre of attention once more; something he enjoyed tremendously, although he was at pains to point out that Holly was by far the more accomplished in almost every respect. Holly, however, stated baldly that just being good at martial arts - or anything else - was no alternative to sheer guts and determination. Everyone was just happy that nobody had been killed, especially Felix. Even all the bad guys had been rounded up and given a fair trial. It really was a completely successful mission.

The wi-fu virus had been eradicated, the supply of *pawaapu* mushrooms[1] had been shut off, and everyone at AIS was looking forward to a nice quiet life with only petty crimes to deal with. At least for now.

In fact, the only problem seemed to be with the party preparations. All the tables were strewn with some sort of downy pollen spikes from willow trees. There were hundreds of them, mostly stacked up in piles on the tables, but a few had got scattered about, and onto the floor. Meanwhile there didn't seem to be anything to wipe your paws with if you got sticky. Jonathan Hart called Ollie over.

---

[1] Just in case we haven't said this already; this is a fictional mushroom. There's no such thing as a pawaapu mushroom, but there are real mushrooms that are very poisonous, like really poisonous, you know, I mean like proper yucky, and they might give you a stomach-ache, or make you puke up all over the place, or even drop down dead, with a bright purple face or something, and we really don't want that to happen. That would be sad! And at least, if you do, we don't want anyone blaming us for it.

"Ollie? You know when I said to make sure there were plenty of napkins on each table?"

"Yes, I made sure tha... Oh!.. *Nap*kins!" Ollie clapped his wing to his head. "I thought you said catkins!" Poor Ollie looked distraught.

"Don't worry, they look quite decorative actually. I'll get some napkins, Ollie," the stag smiled.

* * * * *

M came over to Felix and Holly and told them, "Make the most of today. Next month sees the start of the international private detectives' convention, right here in Wilder Wood."

"Oh no!" Felix exclaimed.

"That sounds like fun," Holly enthused.

M smiled grimly. "We'll see if you feel the same way after a week of them poking their noses into every single case," she said.

"How bad could it be?" Holly wondered aloud.

"You'll see," Felix grumbled.

But not in this book she won't.
Because that's a whole new story.

The End

Also from Blue Poppy Publishing

Teeny Tiny Witch

By Sheila Golding

With 10 full-colour illustrations

by Colin Rowe

It's not easy being the smallest witch on Witch Island. Especially when your spells keep going wrong, and you get banished by the Icy Witch Queen.

Teeny Tiny Witch has enough problems, without having to help a young dragon who misses his mum, or a grumpy wizard who can't do magic.

She especially doesn't want to have to face the Icy Witch Queen again or stand up to a great big bully. But she does all this and more in this charming children's story, which will bewitch adults and children alike.

Includes ten full colour illustrations.

About the author.

Olli hated writing at school. He didn't like being told what to write, and he could never finish before the end of the lesson. Also, his hand hurt from holding a pen, and he made a ridiculous number of mistakes. He spent most lunch-breaks on his own in class, finishing his work.

After leaving school, he went through a variety of jobs but is now more or less a full-time writer. Nobody is more surprised.

The difference was computers. No more holding a pen, and mistakes can easily be corrected. Also, he doesn't have to write what the teacher tells him, and he doesn't have to finish before the bell goes for playtime.

WIN!

About the illustrator

Amii James was chosen to illustrate the first book in this series, “For Cats’ Eyes Only”, from a number of art students at Ilfracombe Academy who submitted work for consideration. She did such a great job on that book that she was automatically chosen to work on this one too.

Amii has been artistic ever since she can remember and studied art at Ilfracombe Academy 6th form, then Petroc College, and is preparing to start university in Sept 2018 with her 3rd professional book on her C.V.

She would like to thank Mr Lawton, head of art at Ilfracombe Academy for his encouragement. Her large, chaotic family have also been a big support, always believing in her and encouraging her to pursue what she loves

Reviews

Please don't forget to review this book.

Authors rely on reviews more than anything else. If you got any pleasure from reading this, then please, please, pretty please, with sugar on top!

Why not do a book review for school? You could use the pictures in a PowerPoint presentation to make it more interesting for the class. We can even send you digital versions of the pictures (possibly in colour) via email if you ask.

If you are able to get a parent or guardian to write a review on Amazon that would be awesome too, but **in your words**. You can also review books on the Blue Poppy Website.

Be honest, if you don't like it, say so but always explain why.

Errm...

Well, this is embarrassing...

So, the thing is... We have a few extra pages to fill up.

You see, this book has to be 128 pages long for technical reasons, and so we ended up with a few extra pages at the end and nothing left to fill them with. We could put loads of adverts for our other books, but if you can't be bothered to check out the "Time Tunnel" series after seeing it in the bit at the beginning of the book then it's hardly going to make much difference if we put it at the end as well is it?

And most of our other books are for adults, such as the excellent "And the Wolf Shall Dwell" by Joni Dee; a gripping espionage thriller, but not suitable for kids.

So for the next few pages there will be some of those silly trivial games you get in comics, just to fill up the space a bit.

N.B. If this is a library book you had better not draw in it, otherwise Cathy will be after you!

"Who's been drawing in this book?"

Help Felix and Holly follow the right monorial track to rescue Aki.
Get it wrong, and Felix ends up behind bars.

Wordsearch

```
v u g p a w a a p u
i b o n i h s h x m
g k y e i k x r o s
g f o c h i a n e a
p t n n l o o o n m
s n t e i r l i a u
a e f g a c m l n r
l c o i z a h i y a
v n l l l b n i p i
a i l l r j q e w r
d v i e a h f s m a
o f e t i k u n a t
r b e n w e i e w d
h a d i r f n s d k
s e n s o d o j i n
```

aki
animal
felix
frida
holly
intelligence
konichiwa
monorail
ninja
ollie
oni
pawaapu
salvador
samurai
sensei
sensodojin
shinobi
tanuki
vincent

How to draw Felix Whiter in 3 easy steps

Step 1. Draw a circle.

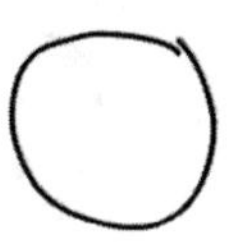

Step 2. Draw some more shapes.

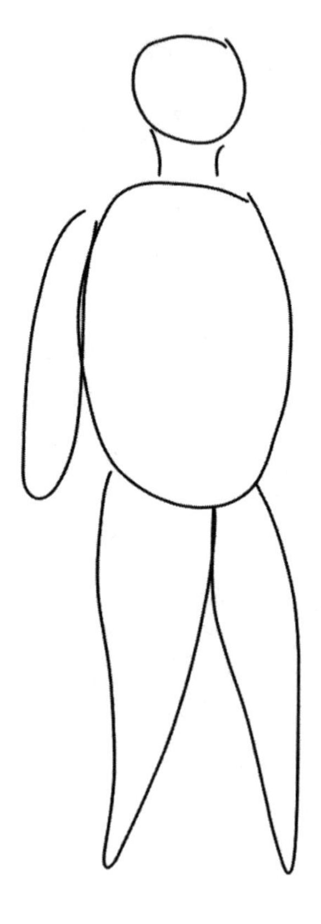

Step 3. Fill in the details.

Now you try...